COUNTRY AND WESTERN

By S.L. Hamilton

VISIT US AT ABDOPUBLISHING.COM

Published by ABDO Publishing Company, 8000 West 78th Street, Suite 310, Edina, MN 55439. Copyright ©2011 by Abdo Consulting Group, Inc. International copyrights reserved in all countries. No part of this book may be reproduced in any form without written permission from the publisher. A&D Xtreme™ is a trademark and logo of ABDO Publishing Company.

Printed in the United States of America, North Mankato, Minnesota.
112010
012011

Editor: John Hamilton
Graphic Design: Sue Hamilton
Cover Design: John Hamilton
Cover Photo: Getty Images
Interior Photos: Alamy-pgs 8, 9, 20 & 32; AP-pgs 6, 7, 18, 19 & 21; Corbis-pgs 10, 11 & 28; Getty Images-pgs 1, 4, 5, 12, 13, 14, 15, 16, 22, 25, 29, 30 & 31; Glow Images-pgs 26 & 27; Jako Jellema-pg 17; Thinkstock-pgs 2, 3, 23, 24 & 25.

Library of Congress Cataloging-in-Publication Data

Hamilton, Sue L., 1959-
  Country and western / S.L. Hamilton.
      p. cm. -- (Xtreme dance)
  ISBN 978-1-61714-730-2
  1. Country-dance. 2. Dance--West (U.S.) I. Title.
  GV1763.H36 2011
  793.3'4--dc22

                    2010037640

CONTENTS

XTREME

COUNTRY AND WESTERN DANCE

Country and western dances go from easygoing and smooth to fast-paced, rollicking fun.

Xtreme Quote

"For the good are always merry. And the merry love the fiddle. And the merry love to dance."

DANCE

Many country and western dances arose from the days of the Old West. At that time, there were many men, but few women. Cowboys, miners, farmers, and ranchers created dances that men could perform individually or with a male partner.

HISTORY

DANCE

Line Dance

A Line Dance is a series of steps performed by individual dancers standing in a line or row. Historically, Line Dancers faced each other or danced following a leader. People all face the same direction in today's Line Dances.

STYLES

Two-Step

The Two-Step grew out of two ballroom dances: Foxtrot and Swing. Once a quick-quick-slow-slow walking step, the modern Two-Step is a fast traveling dance with many turns. People move counter-clockwise around the edge of the dance floor in time to the music.

Square Dance

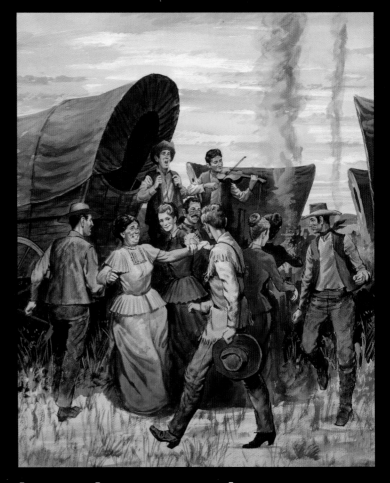

In frontier times, settlers enjoyed dancing. Since people were from many places, few knew the same dance steps. A "caller" began telling dancers what to do. Four couples were organized into a group, forming a square. This began the Square Dance. Today, Square Dances are more complex. However, callers use the same names for the moves.

Xtreme Fact ▶ In 1982, Square Dancing became the national folk dance of the United States.

Jig

Jigs began in Ireland. Varieties of the happy folk dance also became popular in Scotland and England. Jigs were introduced to America by immigrants. A Jig can be performed by one person or many. The Jig requires rapid, lively stamping of the feet, while the upper body stays mostly still.

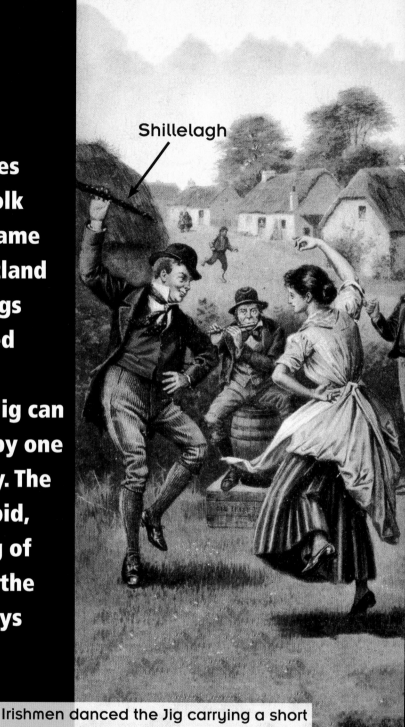

Shillelagh

Reel

Reels are danced in a line with partners facing each other. One of the most popular reels is the Virginia Reel. It is a folk dance that began in Scotland and England. One couple joins hands and sashays down the line and back. The partners then "reel down" by joining elbows and doing a full turn with each person in their partner's line.

Clogging

Clogging is one of the oldest dances known. The steps may be traced to dancers in Africa, as well as many parts of Europe. In the Gaelic language, clog means "time." The dancer's rhythmic tapping goes in time to the music. The sounds are made by the stylized shoes. Historically, clogs were made of wood. Today, they are like a tap shoe, with metal on the bottom of the toes and heels.

Clogging is also called Clog Dancing, Jigging, Flat-Footing, Note Dancing, Buck Dancing, and Foot-Stomping.

Xtreme Fact

XTREME

MOVES

Country and western dances are usually known for their smooth, gliding steps. However, the dance's length and the quickness of the dancer's footwork can be extreme.

DANCE

Country and western dancers wear comfortable clothing. Male and female dancers are often seen in jeans and cotton shirts. Sometimes the shirts are embroidered or fringed.

FASHION

Female dancers also wear jean or prairie skirts. Women who Square Dance wear brightly colored clothing with ruffled petticoats.

Hat and Shoe Styles

Country and western dancers usually wear cowboy hats and boots. They come in a variety of colors and styles. Women who Square Dance wear Mary Janes, low-heeled  shoes with a strap. Cloggers wear a type of tap shoe.

LEARN TO

Many country and western steps are learned from family members who enjoy the dances. Country and western dances are taught at dance halls, schools, and health clubs. Instructional DVDs are also available.

DANCE

DANCE

CONTESTS

Local and national contests are held in the United States, as well as countries around the world. Brazil holds a festival known as Araial de Belô. It includes a popular Square Dance contest.

THE

Caller
A person who calls out the moves in a Square Dance.

Embroider
To sew decorative patterns on a piece of fabric, such as a shirt, using colored threads or yarn.

Foxtrot
A ballroom dance created in the 1920s. The Foxtrot uses two slow and two quick trotting steps. Its moves helped create the country and western Two-Step.

Fringe
A decoration on the edges of country and western shirts or pants where strips of cloth hang down in straight rows.

Gaelic
A language used by the Celts, early settlers of Ireland and Scotland.

GLOSSARY

Old West
A period of time when the western United States was being settled. It is usually associated with the 1800s.

Petticoat
A piece of women's clothing worn underneath a skirt or dress. Female Square Dancers wear brightly colored petticoats trimmed in lace or ruffles.

Sashay
Sideways steps taken while dancing.

Shillelagh
A short wooden stick whirled during a Jig by male dancers in Ireland. It is also used as a weapon. It is pronounced shi-lay-lee.

Swing
A fast-paced dance style with many turns and acrobatic moves. Swing steps inspired the country and western Two-Step.

INDEX